by Turtle

To Mary Kate

BLOOMSBURY CHILDREN'S BOOKS
Bloomsbury Publishing Inc., part of Bloomsbury Publishing Plc
1385 Broadway, New York, NY 10018

BLOOMSBURY, BLOOMSBURY CHILDREN'S BOOKS, and the Diana logo are trademarks of Bloomsbury Publishing Plc

First published in the United States of America in October 2019 by Bloomsbury Children's Books

Bloomsbury books may be purchased for business or promotional use. For information on bulk
purchases please contact Macmillan Corporate and Premium Sales Department at specialmarkets@macmillan.com

Library of Congress Cataloging-in-Publication Data
Names: Wohnoutka, Mike, author, illustrator.
Title: Croc & Turtle: snow fun! / by Mike Wohnoutka ; illustrated by Mike Wohnoutka.
Other titles: Croc and Turtle, snow fun
Description: New York : Bloomsbury, 2019.
Summary: Best friends Croc and Turtle want to play together, but Croc only wants to do exciting things outside in the cold
and Turtle wants to stay safe and warm inside.
Identifiers: LCCN 2019003803 (print) • LCCN 2019006269 (e-book)
ISBN 978-1-68119-637-4 (hardcover) • ISBN 978-1-68119-638-1 (e-book) • ISBN 978-1-68119-639-8 (e-PDF)
Subjects: | CYAC: Best friends—Fiction. | Friendship—Fiction. | Individuality—Fiction. | Crocodiles—Fiction. | Turtles—Fiction.
Classification: LCC PZ7.W81813 Cu 2019 (print) | LCC PZ7.W81813 (e-book) | DDC [E]—dc23
LC record available at https://lccn.loc.gov/2019003803

Art created with Holbein Acryla gouache paint
Typeset in Delima MT Sd
Book design by Danielle Ceccolini
Printed in China by C&C Offset Printing Co., Ltd., Shenzhen, Guangdong
2 4 6 8 10 9 7 5 3 1

All papers used by Bloomsbury Publishing Plc are natural, recyclable products made from wood grown in well-managed forests.
The manufacturing processes conform to the environmental regulations of the country of origin.

To find out more about our authors and books visit www.bloomsbury.com and sign up for our newsletters.

Croc & Turtle

Snow Fun!

Mike Wohnoutka

BLOOMSBURY
CHILDREN'S BOOKS
NEW YORK LONDON OXFORD NEW DELHI SYDNEY

knock
knock

Your list has all
inside things!

Your list has all
outside things!

Outside *or* inside, as long as
we're together, Turtle, I'm happy.

I agree, Croc.
Let's do everything
on *both* lists.

The first thing on my list is:
ice skating.

I don't
know how
to ice skate.

It's easy, Turtle.
Just watch me.

Woooooooooshhhhh!

Isn't outside fun, Turtle?

I'm ready
to go *inside*.

The first thing on *my* list is . . .
CRAFTS!
We're going to make
paper snowflakes.

I'm not very good at
paper snowflakes.

It's easy, Croc.
Just watch me.

I'm ready to go back outside.

The second thing on my list is . . .
sledding!

I can't feel
my toes.

Are you ready, Turtle?
1 . . . 2 . . . 3 . . .

AAAAAAAAAA!

Isn't outside
the best, Turtle?

It's time to
go back inside.

The second
thing on
my list is . . .
do . . . a . . .
PUZZLE!

I can't take it anymore, Turtle.
Inside is too boring!

But, Croc, outside
is too cold and
too dangerous!

I'M
GOING
OUTSIDE!

I'M STAYING INSIDE!

knock
knock

I'm sorry, Turtle. Outside is not as fun without you.

I'm sorry too, Croc. Inside is not as fun without you.

How can we be inside
and outside *and* together?

I have
an idea!

whisper
whisper

This is a great idea, Turtle.

Thanks, Croc.

Here's to being outside . . .

and inside . . .